Search for a clover, discover the world.

Printed June 2012 in China.

Library of Congress Cataloging-in-Publication Data

Heckathorn, Julia
Search for the Hidden Clover: Costa Rica / Julia Heckathorn
Summary: When two children and a kangaroo go searching for a four leaf clover in Costa Rica,
they discover wonders of the natural world that they never knew existed.

ISBN: 978-0-9837010-2-6

Library of Congress Control Number: 2011910494

This book is CPSIA compliant

Photo Credit: Two Toed Sloth Photo on page 15 - ©Judy Avey-Arroyo of the Sloth Sanctuary of Costa Rica, www.slothrescue.org

-To an incredibly talented artist-

To my mother, my artistic inspiration and encouragement.

Be inspired!
www.betzgreen.com

SEARCH FOR THE HIDDEN CLOVER

COSTA RICA

WRITTEN AND ILLUSTRATED BY JULIA HECKATHORN

I went to a place
Where the **land** was **so lush,**
That the leaves hid my face
As I walked through the brush.

The **plants** there were **vast,**
And colorful too!
And there were active volcanoes
Where lava broke through!

The **wildlife** there
Is a sight for eyes **keen.**
Sloths cling to the trees,
Poison Frogs lurk **unseen!**

A beautiful place, so **peacefully serene!**

1

So many **CLOVERS**
With three leaves **to see**,
But there must be a clover
With more leaves than three!

There's a 4-leaf clover on this page! Can you find it?

Your next challenge is to find a 4-leaf clover in Costa Rica!

"There must be a clover
With **four leaves**, not three.
It's hidden here **somewhere**,
But **where** can it be?"

"Let's **walk** past this bridge
And look towards the **ground**.
The ground's where they'll be
If there are **clovers** around."

4

And as we **looked** down,
Guess what we FOUND?
LEAF-CUTTER ANTS
Walking to their ant mound!

SO WE ASKED....

"Would one of you **mind**
Simply **pointing** the way
To any clovers you've **seen**?
We must **find** some today."

⑤

"We're on a tight schedule,
We can't help much **today**.
But a **frog** just hopped by,
Surely he'll lead the way!"

JULIA SAYS

Leaf-cutter Ants are able to carry leaves 20 times the weight of their own bodies!

In a single Leaf-cutter ant colony, you may find **millions of ants** living and working together.

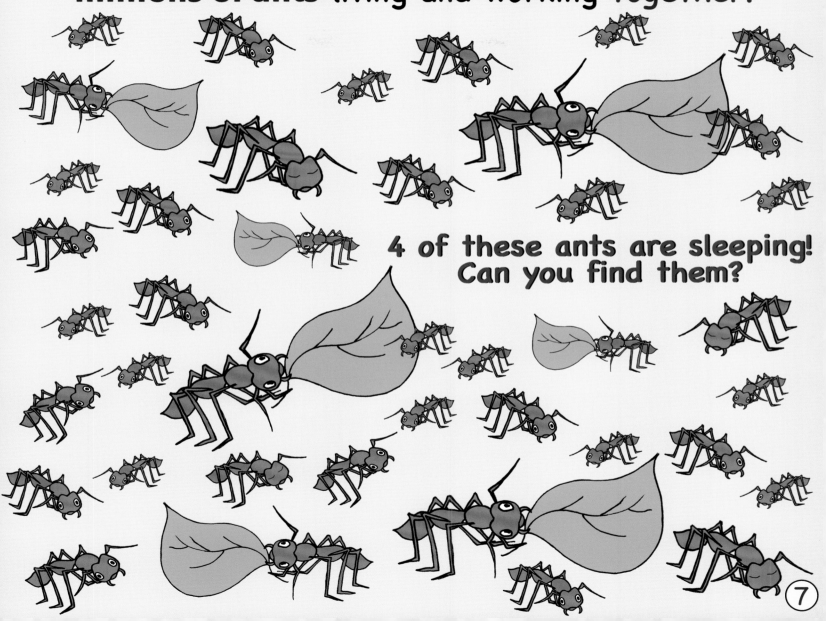

4 of these ants are sleeping! Can you find them?

Then we found a Dart Frog,
Hopping 'round on the ground.
He was green and black,
Sitting on a leaf mound!

JULIA SAYS

How did the Poison Dart Frog get it's name? The poison of these frogs has been placed on the tips of darts for use in hunting!

Do you see the green Poison Dart Frog in the leaves?

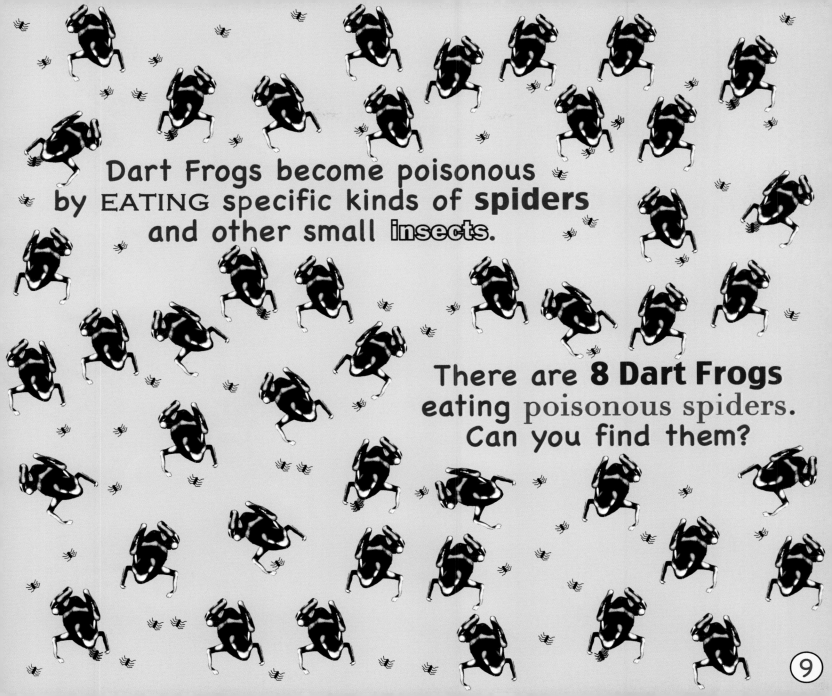

Dart Frogs become poisonous by EATING specific kinds of **spiders** and other small insects.

There are **8 Dart Frogs** eating poisonous spiders. Can you find them?

"I'm **Thumper** the Jumper!
I'm glad that we've met!
There are **no clovers** here,
But don't lose hope yet!"

10

"There's a place down this path,
Where lava once flow.
The soil's so rich,
That clovers must grow!"

"It's just past this brush,
And past the last tree,
By an active volcano!
Come! Follow me!"

11

But as we **walked** further,
We had to say "HI"
To some fuzzy **caterpillars**
As we **swiftly** passed by.

12

"**Good luck** with your mission!
We'll be **thinking** of you!
We're sure you'll find **clovers**!
We **hope** that you do!"

13

These Caterpillars are looking for a leaf to eat!

can you find the 4 caterpillars walking the wrong way?

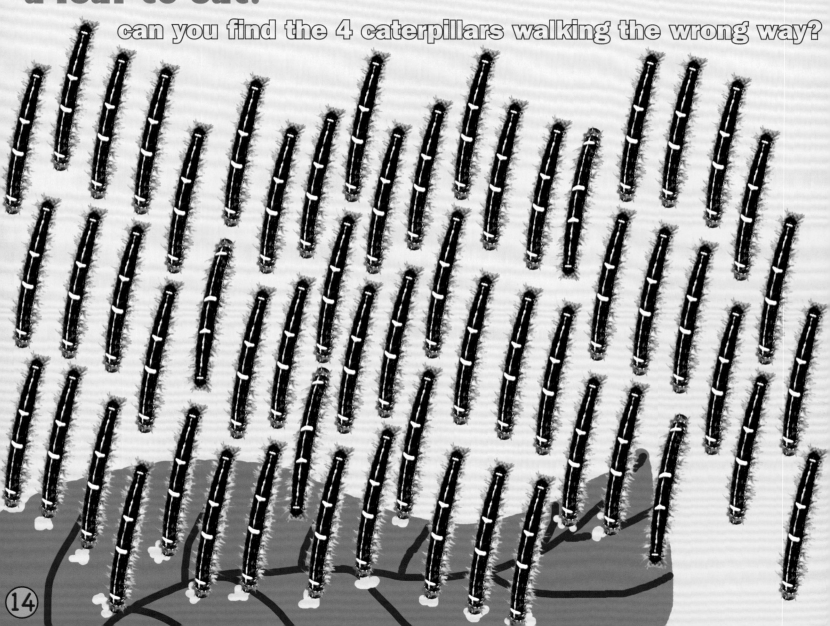

14

We walked toward the clearing,
Where in a low tree,
We found something special,
Oh, but WHAT could it be?

An adult **two-toed sloth**,
With her sloth baby **pup**.
She hung UPSIDE DOWN,
With her pup RIGHT-SIDE UP.

Sloths spend almost all of their time **IN TREES.** Their long claws help them to hold on tight **so that they can** eat, sleep, and play on branches and tree limbs.

Below are two pictures of a Two-Toed Sloth hanging!

There are 4 differences in the pictures. Can you find them?

JULIA SAYS

Two-Toed sloths have 2 toes on their front feet, but just like three-toed sloths, they have 3 toes on their back feet!

"We will have to decline,
We are MUCH TOO SLOW,
But **good luck** everyone!
Thanks for saying HELLO!"

18

Then as we traveled on,
There in our sight,
Was **Arenal Volcano**,
What **beauty**! What **might**!

JULIA SAYS

Arenal Volcano is 7,000 years old! When it erupts, it creates rich, fertile soil that helps vegetation grow!

19

But the land there was **vast**,
We weren't sure where to go,
So we asked a **blue-tailed lizard**
Where clovers might grow.

Costa Rica is home to many different types
of iguanas and other lizards.

Can you find all 5 types of lizards on this page?

"There are **clovers** all over,
You're in the **right** spot!
Let's find clovers with **four leaves**!
We've got a **good** shot!"

22

We found a huge clover patch!

So we LOOKED and we LOOKED
For the most perfect clover,
But they all had THREE leaves,
...So we had to START OVER.

23

Then we saw **MORE** clovers,
And we kept our eyes **peeled**,
For a big 4-LEAF clover,
In this **rich soil field**.

Down on our knees,
We searched through the patch
For a **clover** with four leaves,
And soon, found a **match!!!**

Can you find the 4-leaf clover in this clover patch?

A clover with **four** leaves,
The luckiest kind,
Right in **Costa Rica**,
A fantastic **find**!

THE END

What a great adventure!
What was your favorite part of your Costa Rica journey?

BUT WAIT! THERE'S MORE!

Did you know that caterpillars turn into beautiful moths and butterflies?

The caterpillars we met earlier have many butterfly friends
flying around the pages of this book.

If you didn't see all 6 butterflies, go back now, and try to find them!

AND GET READY TO JOIN US
ON OUR NEXT ADVENTURE
WHEN WE TRAVEL TO A NEW PART OF THE WORLD
IN SEARCH OF ANOTHER 4-LEAF CLOVER!

Help Save the Pygmy Sloths!

There are estimated to be LESS THAN 300
Pygmy Three-Toed Sloths left in the world.

If nothing is done to protect them,
It is projected they will be extinct
within this decade.

The Hidden Clover team is working with conservation groups
to save the species from extinction.

Learn more about our efforts,
and find out how you can help by going to
www.Searchforthehiddenclover.com/pygmysloths

A portion of the proceeds of this book will go towards efforts to save the Pygmy Sloths.

ABOUT HIDDEN CLOVER

Hidden Clover believes that when people go looking for a small piece of nature, they discover the fascinating natural world.

Work on the *Search for the Hidden Clover* book series began in 2009 when
author and illustrator, Julia Heckathorn,
was inspired by the unscathed beauty of forest on a hike to a hidden waterfall.
Julia realized that pictures alone could never sufficiently capture
the true beauty and wonder of nature for young readers.
Thus, Hidden Clover seeks to deliver a perspective changing experience that involves
immersion through books, websites, videos, activities, experiences with nature, and other media.

Julia visits each region of the world presented in her books
to research and photograph before she writes.
This ensures that children get the truest sense of what these natural areas of the world are like.

Hidden Clover seeks to serve children, the community, and the world.
We establish partnerships with preservation organizations to preserve endangered species
and we have pledged to donate a portion of all revenues to these causes.
Julia and her husband also strive to regularly serve in ways such as building wells for clean water
in the jungles of Peru, and taking care of exotic animals
for the enrichment of children who learn through the experience of meeting them.

We hope and pray that we are able to inspire others to love and care for nature in a deeper way.